SEEING STARS!

One Boy's Quest for the Stars of the Sea

WRITTEN AND ILLUSTRATED
BY DONNA ROCKWELL

do.well studio

Reach for the stars!

Donna Rockwell

For Emmett, Shea and Henry, my stars.

Published by Do Well Studio
68 Tupper Road
Sandwich, MA 02563

Printed in the United States of America

First Printing, 2017

ISBN 978-0-692-86200-1

Bulk discounts are available for institutions and non-profit organizations.

www.DoWellStudio.com

Henry, a boy who dreamed of the sea,
came to the seashore with one thing to see.

He had lived his whole life in the mountains, up high,
and the stars that he knew only lived in the sky.

But the stars that he dreamed of were found by the shore.
There he'd find sea stars — or starfish — galore!

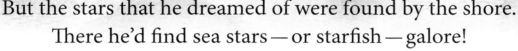

On the very first morning, with a bucket and hope,
he started his search. Did he find any? Nope.

Despite his keen eye, and a wholehearted try,
he didn't see any, and a whole day went by.

Then two and three and four days had passed;
with only one left, Henry had to think fast.

That night, when the moon and the sun traded places
and the stars began showing as faint glowing traces,
Henry did the one thing that he had left to try.
He wished on a star.

(ONE UP IN THE SKY!)

"PLEASE, OH PLEASE— PLEASE, OH PLEASE— PLEASY—PLEASE PLEASE...

...let me see one tomorrow," he said into the breeze.
And although he had little hope left for his dream,
he went straight to bed (even skipping ice cream).

The next morning came even earlier than most,
when he woke to mom screaming like she'd just seen a ghost.

And dad was just standing there, frozen in shock,
his arms stuck in place like a long-broken clock.

Then Henry saw it. Really, how could he not?!
Starfish he wanted?

WELL, STARFISH HE GOT!

They clung to
the steeples...

They covered
the cars...

They stuck to
the lampposts...

...and Sergeant LeMars!

There were hundreds — no, thousands — a massive amount,
in colors and sizes too many to count!

He was stunned and delighted (and a little bit nervous).
Had his one little wish put this town out of service?

The place was in chaos. All the people moved quickly.
"Get them back to the water before they get sickly!"
the Mayor cried out to all who would listen.
But Henry alone saw their strange, magic glisten.

For these were no ordinary stars of the sea;
they were special, as Henry had wished them to be.
He alone knew the secret of the starfish arrival.
He alone knew the certainty of their survival.

Down to the ocean the townspeople raced,
until, in the water, the last one was placed.

The tide picked them up and they went with the flow.
And they ALL made it safely (as you and I know)!

Now Henry left happy.
His dream had come true.
But a new one was forming,
as dreams often do.

As his plane lifted off, he saw something bizarre.
You know, strange things can happen when you wish on a star…

STARFISH FACTS

The Starfish — or Sea Star — may be one of the most beautiful animals in the ocean. Here are a few facts about this magnificent creature.

1. A STARFISH IS NOT A FISH.

It's called an **echinoderm** (a word meaning 'spiny' and 'skin') and is related to sand dollars and sea urchins. Marine scientists are working hard to make the name 'Sea Star' more common, but it's a tough job to rename the Starfish!

2. THEY CAN REGENERATE LIMBS.

It can take a while — up to a year — but if a Starfish loses a **limb** (an arm or leg), it can grow a new one in its place!

3. THEY EAT INSIDE OUT.

When a starfish captures its **prey** (a creature it hunts for food), its stomach comes out through its mouth to digest it, and goes back into its body when it is done. That's one creepy dinner guest!

4. THEY CANNOT SURVIVE IN FRESH WATER
(OR OUT OF WATER — SO ADMIRE THEIR BEAUTY WITH A MASK AND FINS!)

They need to be in water to live, and it has to be **saline water** (salt water). Always. (Unless, of course, there's a touch of starfish magic involved!)

5. THERE ARE OVER 2,000 KINDS OF STARFISH

They live all over the world, in both warm and cold climates. Some **species** (groups of similar living things) have five arms, some have many more—up to 40! They also come in many different colors like red, pink, orange, yellow, green, blue, white, brown, purple and black.

6. A STARFISH HAS NO BRAIN AND NO BLOOD

Starfish use their senses to make decisions. They also use filtered sea water to pump **nutrients** (the ingredients in food that help you grow) through their body.

7. STARFISH ARE SLOOOOOWW!

Even the fastest starfish is a pretty slow mover. The **sand star** (a species of starfish) can travel at a whopping speed of about 9 feet per minute. Some move so slowly the human eye cannot even detect the movement.

8. THEY HAVE QUITE A FEW BIRTHDAYS.

The average age of a starfish in the wild is 35. That's not too bad with so many predators in the ocean! Sea stars have **armor** (a tough, protective covering) on their upper side, and many have prickly spines to keep them from becoming someone's lunch!

A graduate of the Rhode Island School of Design,
Donna Rockwell now paints and lives on Cape Cod
with her husband and three young wish makers.

They all enjoy the stars of the sea and the sky
from the sandy shores they call home.

Thank you to the many friends and family that
supported the creation of this book and to the Sandwich Arts Alliance
for inspiring its creation through its public art project.

Special thanks to Angela D'Allesandro, Laurie Riley and
Linda Conti for their guidance and expertise.

*A portion of the proceeds of this book will be donated to local organizations
dedicated to marine wildlife rescue and education in marine wildlife health and conservation.*

do . well studio

www.DoWellStudio.com